GALAXY ZACK

OPERATION TWIN TROUBLE

By Ray O'Ryan

Illustrated by Jason Kraft

LITTLE SIMON
New York   London   Toronto   Sydney   New Delhi

This book is a work of fiction. Any references to historical events, real people, or real places are used fictitiously. Other names, characters, places, and events are products of the author's imagination, and any resemblance to actual events or places or persons, living or dead, is entirely coincidental.

LITTLE SIMON
An imprint of Simon & Schuster Children's Publishing Division
1230 Avenue of the Americas, New York, New York 10020
First Little Simon paperback edition September 2015
Copyright © 2015 by Simon & Schuster, Inc.
Also available in a Little Simon hardcover edition.
All rights reserved, including the right of reproduction in whole or in part in any form.
LITTLE SIMON is a registered trademark of Simon & Schuster, Inc., and associated colophon is a trademark of Simon & Schuster, Inc.
For information about special discounts for bulk purchases, please contact Simon & Schuster Special Sales at 1-866-506-1949 or business@simonandschuster.com.
The Simon & Schuster Speakers Bureau can bring authors to your live event. For more information or to book an event contact the Simon & Schuster Speakers Bureau at 1-866-248-3049 or visit our website at www.simonspeakers.com.
Designed by Nicholas Sciacca
Manufactured in the United States of America 0815 FFG
1 2 3 4 5 6 7 8 9 10
Library of Congress Cataloging-in-Publication Data
O'Ryan, Ray.
Operation twin trouble / by Ray O'Ryan ; illustrated by Jason Kraft. —
First Little Simon paperback edition.
pages cm. — (Galaxy Zack ; #12)
Summary: "Zack's twin sisters are best friends, but when the two get into an argument while visiting another planet, Zack finds himself stuck in the middle of a tricky twin situation"— Provided by publisher.
ISBN 978-1-4814-4400-2 (hc) — ISBN 978-1-4814-4399-9 (pbk) —
ISBN 978-1-4814-4401-9 (eBook)
[1. Science fiction. 2. Twins—Fiction. 3. Sisters—Fiction.
4. Brothers and sisters—Fiction. 5. Friendship—Fiction.
6. Human-alien encounters—Fiction.]
I. Kraft, Jason, illustrator. II. Title.
PZ7.O7843Op 2015
[Fic]—dc23
2015006939

CONTENTS

Chapter 1

Game Time!

Zack Nelson stood in the living room of his house on the planet Nebulon. He stared at his friend Drake Taylor.

Zack's parents, Shelly and Otto, sat on their floating shimmer-couch. Zack's twin sisters, Charlotte and Cathy, sat nearby on the floor.

It was family game night at the Nelson house. Three teams were playing Space Charades. Zack and Drake were one team. Charlotte and Cathy were another. And their parents were the third team.

"Ready . . ."

". . . Set . . ."

". . . Go!" the girls shouted together.

A hologram of a digital timer appeared in the air. It was projected by Iiu, the Nelson's Indoor Robotic Assistant. The timer started counting off the seconds.

Zack pinned his arms at his sides. He began to jump up and down.

"Jump!" guessed Drake.

Zack shook his head.

"Fly! Leap! High! Ceiling!"

Zack kept shaking his head.

"Bounce!" Drake shouted.

Zack stopped jumping and cupped his hand behind his ear.

"Sounds like bounce?"

Next, Zack held his hands together over his head.

"Circle?" guessed Drake. "Zero? . . .
The letter O?"

Zack touched his nose, the sign that
Drake was correct.

"Bounce-O-what?"

Zack pretended he had a shovel in his hands and was digging in the ground.

"Dig? Shovel?"

Zack shook his head. He pretended to throw something into the imaginary hole he had dug. Then he went back to his shoveling.

"Bury!" shouted Drake.

Again, Zack touched his nose.

"Bounce-O-Bury," Drake said. He thought for moment.

"Boingoberry!" he shouted.

"That's it!" yelled Zack. He gave Drake a high five.

Boingoberries grew all over Venus. They were used to make Zack's favorite shake and syrup.

Drake looked at the timer hologram. "One minute and thirty seconds," he announced. "Pretty good."

"Okay, girls. Your turn," Zack said, taking a seat in his invisible energy chair. He appeared to be sitting on thin air.

The girls stood up. They both had flaming red hair. Charlotte kept hers in a ponytail. She also wore a scarf around her neck. Cathy wore her hair in two braided pigtails. This was the only way most people could tell them apart.

"Ready, set, go!" Zack shouted.

Charlotte stuck out her left hand. She then pretended to strum a guitar with her right hand.

"TBD!" Cathy shouted.

"That's it!" Charlotte said. She glanced up at the timer and cheered.

"Five seconds! That's a new record!"
Zack exclaimed from his invisible
chair. "TBD? That's not even a word!"

"Shows what you know. TBD is . . ."

". . . our favorite band. It stands for . . ."

". . . Twin Boys Dancing!"

"No fair," Zack moaned. "How can we compete against two people who do everything together? They even talk like one person."

"I have heard of TBD," said Drake. "In fact, I read that they are playing a concert on their home planet, Mirer."

The girls ran over to their parents.

"Can we . . ."

". . . go . . ."

". . . please?"

"Well," said Mrs. Nelson, "I guess that would be okay."

"Yay!" the girls screeched.

Mr. Nelson scratched his head. "But what about our turn at Space Charades?"

Chapter 2

Journey to Mirer

The space cruiser carrying Zack and his family lifted off from the Creston City Spaceport. They were on their way to the planet Mirer.

The view outside changed from blue sky to black space. Thousands of stars twinkled in the darkness.

"You know, Mom, every time I travel in space, it's just as exciting as the first time," said Zack.

"I know how much you love it, honey," said Mom. "It almost doesn't matter where you are going."

In the seats next to Zack, Charlotte and Cathy could not hold in their excitement.

"I can't believe . . ."

". . . we are going to see . . ."

". . . TBD!" the girls squealed with delight.

"Uh-huh," said Zack. He turned back to his window.

"I take it you're not looking forward to the TBD concert, Captain?" asked Dad.

"No, but I am looking forward to seeing a new planet," Zack said.

"And, when I get home, I can add a 3-D image of Mirer to my holographic planet-collector."

Charlotte and Cathy kept talking about their favorite band.

"I hope they sing . . ."

". . . 'Double Trouble.' Oooooh, that's my . . ."

". . . favorite song! *There are two of us. No, you're not seeing double . . .*"

". . . *Take us as we are, or there's gonna be trouble!*" the girls sang loudly, then shrieked with excitement.

A short while later an announcement came over the ship's speakers.

"Passengers, we are beginning our landing pattern for Mirer."

"TBD, here . . ."

". . . we . . ."

". . . COME!!!"

A few minutes later the space cruiser
landed. Zack walked down the ramp
from the ship. He couldn't believe what
he saw. He rubbed his eyes.

"Am I seeing double?" he asked.
"There are two of everything!"

23

Chapter 3

Mirer, Mirer

Zack looked around the Mirer City Spaceport. Mirens looked very much like humans, except that their skin was orange. But Zack had met many aliens since he and his family moved from Earth to Nebulon. Seeing people who looked different was no big deal.

What was a big deal was the fact that every person walking through the spaceport had a twin! Everyone.

"Mommy, can we please have . . ."

". . . four mirlars so we can buy . . ."

". . . a Double-Crunch Duo Bar to share?" said two little boys as they walked past Zack.

"Oh no!" he cried. "Everyone here talks like my sisters!"

The Nelsons reached the flying-car rental area. Dad spoke with the two identical clerks behind the counter.

"We need a car for the five of us," he said.

"Five?" the two clerks said together.
They looked right at Zack.

"Your twin couldn't . . ."

". . . make it today? I'm sorry, you
must be . . ."

". . . very lonely," the clerks said.

"I don't have a twin," Zack replied.

The two clerks looked at each other in shock.

Zack thought about how Charlotte and Cathy often felt different from everyone else because they were twins. Here in Mirer, he was starting to understand how they felt.

"Here's our car!" said Dad a few seconds later. "Or should I say 'cars'?"

The Nelsons climbed into a car. It had two windshields, two trunks, four headlights, and two sets of seats.

"This looks like two cars glued together!" said Zack.

With everyone in, the Nelsons zoomed out of the spaceport. Zack looked around at Mirer City, the capital of the planet. This was where the TBD concert would take place that evening. They had all day to tour the city.

31

"There are two of every building!"
Zack said. "Every building has a twin
standing right next to it!"

First, the Nelsons stopped at the
Mirer City Zoo. As Zack walked around,
he saw a whole bunch of animals he
had never heard of.

"Quarnaks," Zack said, reading the first sign. "Four-legged creatures with fur and wings. And there are two of them!"

"Mumbrads," he said, reading the next sign. Two identical huge green beasts stood side by side. "They look like an elephant crossed with a hippo and a rhino!"

"I love . . ."

". . . this zoo! There are two . . ."

". . . of everything!" said the girls.

Zack suddenly noticed the sky getting darker. He looked up and saw gray clouds moving in front of Mirer's two suns.

Rain started pouring down. The Nelsons ran for cover in the zoo's snack shack.

"Since we're here," said Dad, rubbing his hands together, "who wants a snack?"

"We do!" Charlotte and Cathy
shouted together.

"Me too," said Zack. He glanced at
the menu.

"A Double-Dual-Ice-Cream Planet,"
he said. "I want one of those. Or should
I say . . . two of those!"

Zack's snack arrived. His eyes opened wide. The bowl was black, covered in white dots that looked like stars. In the bowl were two huge scoops of ice cream. Bright orange marshmallows orbited around the ice cream "planets" like tiny moons.

Outside, thunder cracked and lightning flashed. Zack looked out the window. Every lightning flash contained two jagged white bolts.

"Even the lightning here comes in pairs!" said Zack. Then he shoved another spoonful of ice cream into his mouth.

A few minutes later, the rain slowed down. The clouds began to break up, and sunlight poured through. There in the sky, a double rainbow appeared.

"This is the coolest planet . . ."

". . . in the galaxy!"

"Twins rule!" the girls cheered.

Chapter 4

Twin Boys Dancing!

The Nelsons spent the rest of the day touring Mirer City. Zack couldn't get over the fact there were two of everything. Kids in the park played a version of soccer—with two balls at once. Others rode jet-powered hoverboards—one for each foot!

Dinner at the Double Down Diner
was twin galactic patties. "At least they
have food I like here—even if it is just
two patties on two buns," said Zack.

For dessert Zack had a mondo-
chocolate layercake—two cakes, four
layers each. The twins shared a helping
of doubleberry pie. Doubleberries grew
throughout Mirer, and always in pairs.

After dinner, it was finally time for the concert.

"Twin . . ."

". . . Boys . . ."

". . . Dancing! Here we come!" the girls shouted.

The Nelsons drove to the arena where the concert was going to take place. It was called the Dual Dome.

Zack looked up at two round domes rising from a flat platform. "This place looks like a big, bald, two-headed monster," he said.

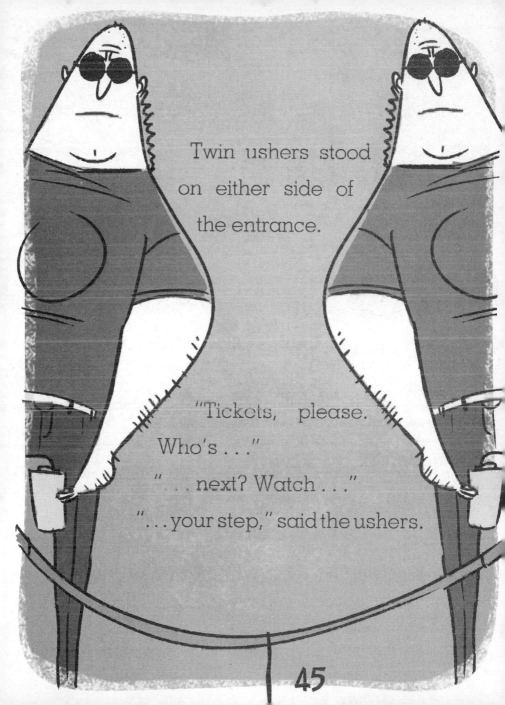

Twin ushers stood
on either side of
the entrance.

"Tickets, please.
Who's . . ."
" . . . next? Watch . . ."
" . . . your step," said the ushers.

A few minutes later, Zack, the twins, and his parents were in their seats. The lights went down and the crowd cheered.

Then a voice boomed from the arena's giant speakers. "Twins of all ages! Please welcome Mirer's own Twin . . . Boys . . . Dancing!"

The Twin Boys burst onto the stage. Of course, they were wearing identical outfits. Tiny rows of colored lights blinked across their shirts. Lasers flashed from their boots. They each grabbed a microphone and launched into their first song: "Double Crush!"

"No matter what you do . . ."

"... *you can count from one to two ...*"

"... *but still it will be true ...*"

"... *I've got a double crush on you!*"

Charlotte and Cathy sang along with every word. The also imitated the hand movements that the boys made. Before the song was over, they were

up and dancing. So was every other
girl in the place.

Zack's parents bobbed their
heads in time with the music. They
were glad that the girls were having
so much fun.

Zack, on the other hand, was bored
out of his mind.

These guys have nothing on Retro Rocket! he thought. Retro Rocket was Zack's favorite band from Earth. He began thinking about intermission, when he could go see what double-size snacks were for sale.

After several songs, a spotlight started moving across the audience.

"Okay, girls . . ."

". . . this is the part of the show . . ."

". . . when one lucky fan gets to dance with us on stage!" the boys shouted.

The crowd went wild.

Cries of "Pick me!" echoed throughout the arena.

Suddenly, the spotlight stopped. It landed right on Charlotte!

"Come up, little lady, and . . ."

". . . dance with . . ."

"Twin   Boys . . . Dancing!"

Charlotte jumped from her seat and ran toward the stage. Cathy jumped up too, running close behind her sister.

Charlotte reached the stage. One of the Twin Boys leaned down and offered her a hand. Two security guards stepped out right in front of Cathy.

"I'm sorry. Only one guest . . ."

". . . is allowed on the stage," said the security guards.

"But I'm her sister!" Cathy cried. The guards looked back toward the stage. Charlotte was dancing with the Twin Boys.

"It looks like she's doing . . ."

". . . just fine by herself," said the guards.

"Now please go back to your seat."

Cathy was crushed. She had never been jealous of anyone in her life. And now she was jealous of her own sister! She walked slowly back to her family.

Up onstage, Charlotte danced, holding hands with the boys. A huge smile beamed from her face.

"Now this is great, isn't it?" Dad said to Cathy.

Cathy said nothing. She sat with her arms crossed. She wished she was up onstage in Charlotte's place.

Chapter 5
Long Ride Home

Following the concert, the Nelsons boarded the space cruiser for the ride home. Charlotte could not stop talking about her time onstage.

"And then they twirled me around and around," she said excitedly. "And just when I thought I might fall, the

Twin Boys lifted me into the air! And everyone cheered—for me!"

Zack quickly realized two things. First, he was really getting tired of hearing about the concert. And second, he could not remember the last time that he heard one of the twins complete a sentence by herself.

"That's wonderful, honey," said Mom. She smiled at Charlotte, then looked over at Cathy. Cathy stared down at the floor between her feet and frowned. Mom was happy for Charlotte. But she was worried about Cathy, who was obviously feeling left out.

"I'm going to go to the snack machine," Zack announced. "Be right back."

"I'll go with you," said Cathy.

Zack and Cathy headed to the back of the ship. Once they were away from the rest of their family, Cathy turned to her brother.

"It's not fair," she complained. "Not fair at all!"

"What's not fair?" asked Zack.

"Charlotte got to go onstage, but I didn't," she said. "I mean, just because we look alike doesn't mean we are the same person."

"You could have fooled me," said Zack. He couldn't resist giving his sister a hard time.

"Well, we're not!" Cathy shouted. "We are two *different* people!"

Zack could not recall the last time he had a conversation this long with only one of his sisters.

Zack and Cathy arrived at the snack machine. The choices included brick bark, crispy fritters, and nebu-nuts. While they were deciding, a tall girl near the snack machine stood up and pointed at Cathy. "Hey, look, everybody. It's the girl who got to dance with TBD!" she said.

63

Cathy smiled for the first time all day. *Maybe I can get a little bit of the attention*, she thought. *No one will know that it wasn't me up on that stage.*

But just as Cathy opened her mouth, Charlotte stepped up to the snack machine.

"Actually, I was the one dancing with TBD," she said.

Cathy looked super-annoyed. "You couldn't even pretend it was me for one minute?" she asked.

"Well, it wasn't you—it was me!" replied Charlotte.

It was strange to see his sisters argue, but Zack was kind of enjoying this surprising trouble in twinland.

Chapter 6

Shopping Spree

The next morning, Zack hurried downstairs.

"Good morning, Master Just Zack," said Ira. "Would you like your usual breakfast?"

"You bet! Thanks, Ira," said Zack.

"Preparing nebu-cakes," said Ira.

"And don't forget the boingoberry syrup!" said Zack.

A moment later a steaming stack of nebu-cakes slid out of an opening in the kitchen counter. As Zack gobbled up his breakfast, Charlotte came downstairs. Cathy followed a few seconds later.

"Good morning, Charlotte. Good morning, Cathy," said Ira. "Would you

both like your usual bowl of Cosmic Crispies?"

"Sure. Thanks, Ira," said Charlotte. She was still beaming from her time onstage with TBD.

"No," said Cathy. "If she's having that, then I want something else. I'll have nebu-cakes, like Zack."

Charlotte glared at her sister.

"Well, if she's not having our usual

breakfast, I won't either," she said. "I'll have a bowl of Astro-Flakes."

Mom burst into the kitchen.

"Who wants to go to Cisnos for a quick shopping trip?" she asked, smiling.

"I do!" cried Cathy.

"Me too!" said Charlotte.

"Sure," said Zack. "I finally have enough on my allowance card to get that retro remote-control space cruiser!" He raced to get his card.

"Well, hurry up, girls, and finish your breakfast," said Mom. "Then go and brush your teeth."

After speeding through breakfast— Cathy had nebu-cakes and Charlotte had Astro-Flakes—the girls went to get ready.

A few seconds later, Zack and his mom heard a shriek from upstairs. They rushed to see what had happened.

"Look at this!" Charlotte cried. She held up a shredded scrap of clothing. "Luna chewed up my favorite scarf!"

Luna, the Nelson's dog, was still chomping on a piece of the scarf.

"Now no one will be able to tell me apart from Cathy."

"Why don't we get you a new scarf?" Mom suggested.

"If *she* gets something new to wear, *I* want something new to wear too!" said Cathy.

"Of course, honey," said Mom.

73

Zack rolled his eyes and headed downstairs. After a short space flight, Zack, Mom, and the twins arrived at the Cisnos Mondo-Mall.

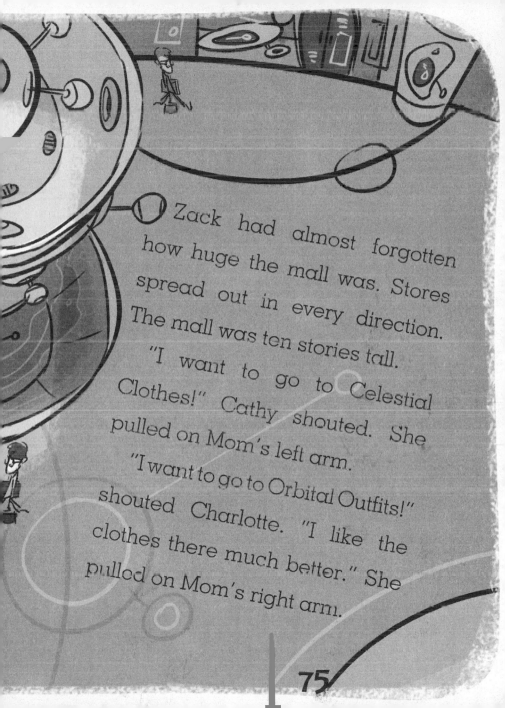

Zack had almost forgotten how huge the mall was. Stores spread out in every direction. The mall was ten stories tall.

"I want to go to Celestial Clothes!" Cathy shouted. She pulled on Mom's left arm.

"I want to go to Orbital Outfits!" shouted Charlotte. "I like the clothes there much better." She pulled on Mom's right arm.

"I'll see you guys later," said Zack. He wanted to get as far away from his stressed sisters as possible.

Zack remembered that the Mondo-Mall had Midge—the Mall Interactive Directory Guide Escort. It helped shoppers find whatever they were looking for. It also guided family members back to a meeting point when they were finished shopping.

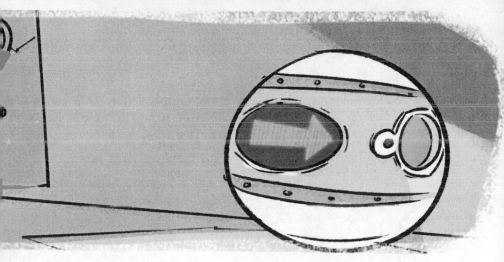

"Midge, where can I find the retro remote-control space cruiser?" asked Zack.

A small round metal ball appeared, floating in the air.

"I am Midge," said a voice coming from a speaker on the flying ball. "I am here to help you. Simply follow your name, Zack."

Zack's name appeared on the floor.

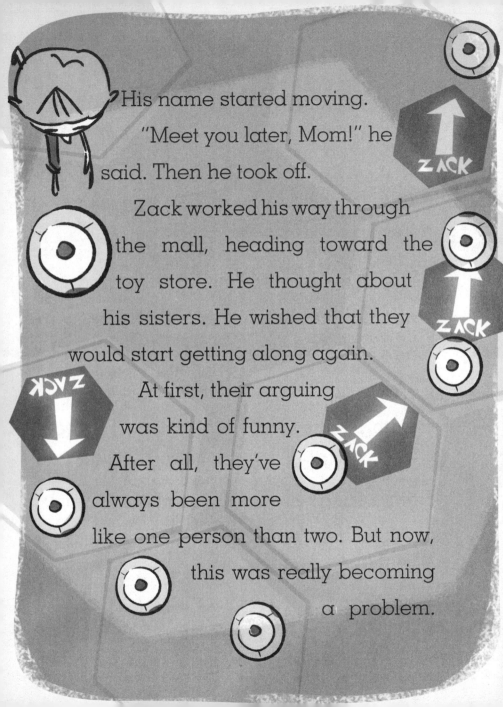

His name started moving.

"Meet you later, Mom!" he said. Then he took off.

Zack worked his way through the mall, heading toward the toy store. He thought about his sisters. He wished that they would start getting along again.

At first, their arguing was kind of funny.

After all, they've always been more like one person than two. But now, this was really becoming a problem.

And Zack saw that it really bothered
Mom. Maybe *he* could fix the problem!

It was time for: Operation Twin
Trouble!

Chapter 7
Operation Twin Trouble

Zack finally arrived at Terrifically Tremendous Toys, the biggest toy store in the Mondo-Mall.

"Wow!" he said, looking around at the cool gadgets. He saw a jet pack, a robot, a holographic car, and so many other incredible toys.

Zack wanted everything. But this store was very expensive. It took him weeks to save up enough for the retro remote-control space cruiser. But it only took a few seconds to find it.

Zack grabbed one of the boxes and headed to the counter to pay.

"Thank you for shopping at our Terrifically Tremendous Toys," said the sales clerk. "As a bonus, everyone who buys a toy today gets a free Cosmic Karen doll."

Maybe this doll can help bring my sisters back together, Zack thought. Operation Twin Trouble is underway.

"Thanks," he said to the clerk. Zack hurried out of the store.

"Midge, please take me to my mom and sisters," he said.

"Certainly," said Midge. Zack's name appeared on the floor.

Midge led Zack to the Orbital Outfits clothing store. He found his mom slouched in a chair. She looked exhausted.

"How's the shopping going, Mom?" Zack asked.

Before Mom could answer, Charlotte popped out of a dressing room. Cathy stepped out of the dressing room next-door.

Charlotte was wearing a new scarf and a long skirt with flowers that moved. They looked as if they were blowing in a gentle breeze.

Cathy, on the other hand, wore a pair of jeans covered in what looked like soft fur.

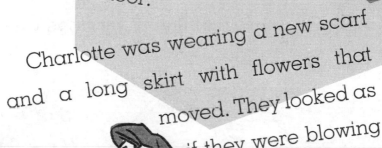

"My skirt is so much cooler than your jeans," said Charlotte.

"No way!" Cathy shouted. "My jeans are as soft as Luna's fur!"

"Girls, really," Mom said. "Can't you both have nice outfits? Why does one have to be better?"

"I think I have a way to make both of you happy," said Zack. He pulled the Cosmic Karen doll from his bag. "A brand-new Cosmic Karen doll!"

Cathy snatched the doll out of Zack's hands. She gave him a big hug.

"Thanks, Zack," she squealed. "You are best brother ever!"

Charlotte grabbed the doll and tried to yank it away from Cathy.

"Obviously, Zack got the doll for me, not you!" Charlotte said. She pulled hard. One of Cosmic Karen's arms snapped right off.

"That's enough," said Mom. "You girls need to share."

"I'm tired of sharing everything just because we're twins!" both girls said angrily.

Operation Twin Trouble is off to a shaky start, thought Zack.

Chapter 8
Phase Two

Back at home, Zack decided to work extra hard to help his sisters be friends again. He found Cathy in her room.

"Remember how I used to joke about you and Charlotte finishing each other's sentences?" he asked.

"Yeah," said Cathy.

"Well, now I miss that," said Zack.
"I think it would be great if you two got
along again."

"Why should we?" asked Cathy.

"Well, you are sisters," said Zack.
"You've been together every minute of
your life for eleven years. Doesn't that
count for something?"

"Yeah, it counts for lots of time I wasted," said Cathy.

"But you've always liked to play together," said Zack. "Like, all the dolls you've shared."

"If they are dolls that she liked, I don't want them!" said Cathy.

She went into her closet and pulled out a big box of dolls. She sorted through them, handing some to Zack.

"I don't want this one . . . or this one . . . or, oh, this one was her favorite," said Cathy. "She can have all of these. Just give them to her."

Zack's arms were full of dolls. The pile reached up to his nose. He had to look over it to see where he was going.

Zack stumbled downstairs, bumping into walls. He tried not to drop the stack of dolls. Even Luna had to help him. Charlotte was sorting through piles of clothes in the Nelson's playroom.

"What are those?" Charlotte asked.

"These are dolls that Cathy thought you might like," said Zack. He knew that this was not exactly what Cathy had said. But he hoped that the dolls could bring some peace between the sisters.

Charlotte leaned in close to her brother. "If they were hers, I don't want them!" she said.

Zack took a step back and tripped over a pile of clothes on the floor. He fell back. The dolls scattered all over the room.

"I'm getting rid of all my clothes that are the same as Cathy's," Charlotte said.

She gathered up a big bundle and shoved the clothes into Zack's arms.

"Here, I don't want to wear these anymore," said Charlotte. "Give them to Cathy.

Once again Zack had his arms full with a pile that nearly covered

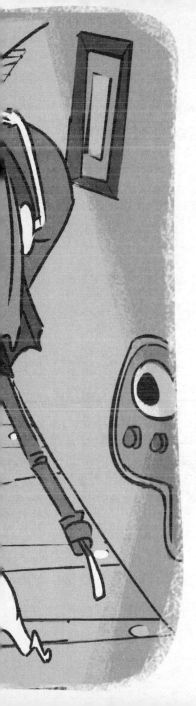

his eyes. Stumbling back upstairs, he went to Cathy's room.

"What are you holding?" Cathy asked.

"Clothes that Charlotte thought you would like," Zack said. He hoped this plan, which didn't work so well on Charlotte, might work on Cathy.

No such luck.

"I don't want these outfits if they came from her!" shouted Cathy.

She quickly pulled out a shirt from the bottom of the pile in Zack's arms. The whole bundle of clothing tumbled to the floor.

"I don't want any of this stuff," said Cathy.

Zack went to his room. He laid down on his bed. Luna sat beside him.

"I don't know what to do, Luna," he said, scratching her head. "I'm exhausted from going back and forth, trying to patch things up. And nothing I do seems to work, Operation Twin Trouble is a failure!"

Chapter 9
The Longest Dinner

That night at dinner, Zack sat between Charlotte and Cathy. They had always sat next to each other. Since returning from Mirer, they had been sitting apart. And they refused to speak to each other.

"Zack, can you ask my sister to pass the peas?" Cathy said.

"Charlotte, can you pass the peas?"
Zack asked.

Charlotte handed the bowl of peas
to Zack. He then passed it on to Cathy.

*Maybe this might help bring them
together,* Zack secretly hoped.

"Zack, will you ask my sister to pass
the bread?" Charlotte said.

"Cathy, can you pass the bread?" Zack asked.

"Zack, can you tell my sister that I haven't taken my piece of bread yet," said Cathy.

"Zack, can you tell my sister that she has had the bread for half the meal," said Charlotte. "Tell her she should learn to share."

"Me? Learn to share?" shouted Cathy. "I'm not the one who got to dance with TBD."

"Girls, I do wish you would try to get along," said Mom. "Just the other day you were working together as a great team when we were playing Space Charades."

Maybe that's it, thought Zack. *Maybe playing a game can bring them back together!*

"Speaking of Space Charades," Zack said, "why don't we play after dinner? I can ask Drake to come by."

"That's a wonderful idea, Zack," said Mom.

"Absolutely," Dad agreed. "Especially since Mom and I didn't get our turn last time!"

"I'll play, as long as Cathy is not on my team," said Charlotte.

"I call dibs on Zack," said Cathy.

"Good. I call dibs on Drake," said Charlotte.

This was not what Zack had in
mind. Still, at least the girls would be
playing the same game. He grabbed
his hyperphone and sent a message
to Drake.

Chapter 10

Teamwork

After dinner Drake arrived. He joined the Nelsons in the living room for a game of Space Charades.

Mom and Dad went first.

Mom took her index finger and her middle finger and made a cutting motion.

"Cut? Chop. Snip?"

Mom shook her head, then repeated the motion.

"Scissors!" Dad shouted.

Mom touched her nose. The she started shaking her head.

"Head? Shake? Ummm . . . No!"

Mom touched her nose.

"Scissor-know," said Dad. "Scissor know? Cisnos!" he shouted.

"You got it," said Mom.

Cathy read the floating timer. "Fifty-one seconds," she said. "Our turn."

Cathy and Zack stood up. Zack
began.

He pretended to put food into his
mouth.

"Eat? Chew? Taste?"

Zack shook his head.

He repeated the eating gesture, then pointed at his hand.

"Finger? Food? Fork? Knife? Spoon?"

Zack touched his nose.

"Spoon . . . spoon something."

Next, Zack opened his mouth and pressed his finger on his tongue.

"Mouth . . . tongue . . . Argh! I don't know. You are terrible at this game."

Zack kept trying. The timer passed
two minutes, then three, then four.

Cathy threw her hands up in
frustration. "I give up."

"I was going for 'aah' like you say
when the doctor looks at your throat,"
Zack explained. "Spoon-aah."

"What is 'spoon-aah'?"

"Sounds like 'Luna.' I was going for 'Luna.'"

"All you had to do was pretend you were a dog," said Cathy. "I would have gotten it in two seconds."

Charlotte and Drake were next. They didn't do much better.

Drake was trying to act out the word "hyperphone," but all his clues left Charlotte staring at him blankly. In the end Charlotte gave up too.

"I guess Mom and I are the winners," said Dad.

"That's because . . ."

". . . boys are really bad at . . ."

". . . playing Space Charades."
Charlotte and Cathy said.

They looked at each other for a
second. They had not finished each
other's sentences in days.

The girls both smiled.

"Let's play again. This time . . ."

". . . it's the boys . . ."

". . . against the girls!"

"You got it!" said Zack. He was thrilled that the girls were getting along again. And he had never been so excited about losing a game.

GALAXY ZACK

ADVENTURE!

HERE'S A SNEAK PEEK!

Zack Nelson stood in front of his house on the planet Nebulon. He was waiting for the Sprockets Speedybus to pick him up to go to Sprockets Academy.

Suddenly, a silver blur appeared in the distance.

There's the bus, he thought.

An excerpt from *Science Fair Disaster!*

The blur stopped right in front of Zack. The bus doors opened and he climbed on board.

The bus was filled with kids talking and laughing. As Zack headed toward the back, he overheard a bunch of conversations.

"My idea is to build a robot that can play galactic blast with you *and* transform into a hover car to take you anywhere you want to go," said a boy.

"I am going to build a machine that recycles garbage into clean fuel," said a girl. "Then I am use that fuel for my hyper-ener-verter to power my house."

An excerpt from *Science Fair Disaster!*

"My radioactive Surge-a-Matron will shrink atoms even smaller," said another boy as Zack walked past.

Zack spotted his friend Drake Taylor. Drake was busy scribbling on his electro-note-screen with his finger.

Zack sat down next to him.

"What's going on?" asked Zack. "When did everyone at Sprockets Academy become so interested in science?"

Drake looked up. "Ever since this morning when Sprockets was picked to host the Intergalactic Science Fair!" he said excitedly.

An excerpt from *Science Fair Disaster!*